# TOBY
## THE TORTOISE
### Gerald Durrell

*Illustrated by Keith West*

*Arcade Publishing / New York*

LITTLE, BROWN AND COMPANY

When I was young, I was lucky enough to live on an island, an island called Corfu in Greece. It was a very beautiful island, and we lived in a big white house surrounded by forests of olive trees. In these forests lived lots of curious animals such as various kinds of lizards, frogs, toads, and snakes, and any number of interesting insects, from beautifully colored butterflies to fat, hairy spiders and furry blue bumblebees. Many other creatures lived in the warm blue sea that surrounded the island: strange fishes, brightly colored shellfish, crabs, lobsters, and octopuses.

All these animals were my friends. I used to collect them as pets, and they would come and live in my house with me in special cages I built for them. So I always had many different kinds of creatures sharing my bedroom and the big verandah that ran along one side of the house.

My favorite pet was my dog, Roger. He was a big dog with thick, curly black fur, large brown eyes, and a stumpy tail that he wagged very fast when he was pleased. Roger slept in a basket in my room, and he always used to wake up early and try to persuade me to take him for a walk. He would stretch and yawn and then come across to my bed and lick my hand to wake me up. Then he would growl, "Come on, come on. Wake up. I want to go for a walk."

"Oh, Roger," I would yawn. "Why do you have to wake me up so early, when I was having a lovely sleep?"

Roger didn't think five o'clock was early. He knew the sun was up, the sky was blue, the birds were all singing, and it was a beautiful day, not one for lying in bed.

So I would get up and dress, and Roger and I would go off into the olive trees to see what we could find.

One day when we were on one of these early morning walks, we had a very exciting adventure. We were walking along some cliffs by the sea when suddenly Roger stopped and cocked his head to one side, as if he were listening to something.

"What is it?" I asked. "I don't hear anything."

Roger bounded on ahead, and suddenly I could hear what his sharp ears had heard — a tiny voice shouting, "Help! Help! Please help me or I'm going to drown!"

We ran along the cliffs, peering down, and soon we saw who was in trouble. It was a tortoise. He had fallen into the blue sea and was in danger of drowning, for land tortoises can't swim.

"Help! Help!" he was crying in panic.

"Don't worry," I shouted. "We'll rescue you."

On our walks we always carried jars and boxes for the insects we found and a rope that we used for climbing trees or cliffs. Now I unwound the rope, tied one end around a strong olive tree, and let the rest of it hang over the cliff. Going down the cliff was easy, and I was soon dangling on the rope close to the water. I waited until a small wave pushed the tortoise close to me, and then I grabbed him and held him against my chest.

"Oh, thank you so much," he said, his voice muffled against my shirt. "I felt sure no one would rescue me."

"Well, you're safe now," I said, starting to climb up the rope, "but how did you manage to get into the sea?"

"Well," said the tortoise, "wild strawberries are my favorite fruit. I was walking along the cliff, and I saw some growing on the very edge. I rushed forward to eat them, but a bit of the cliff gave way, and before I knew what was happening, I was in the sea."

When we got to the top of the cliff, we sat down to have a rest, for climbing up the rope had been difficult.

"What's your name?" asked Roger.

"Toby," said the tortoise. "I'm named after my father."

"Tell me, Toby," I asked. "Would you like to come and live at my house for a while? There are lots of other animal friends of ours there, and we would give you nice things to eat."

"Will I have wild strawberries?" asked Toby.

"Yes," I said, "as many as you can eat."

"And you'll be just in time for my birthday party," said Roger. "I'll be five years old next week."

"Oh, what fun," cried Toby. "I'm so glad you rescued me!"

So we went off home, and I carried Toby, since he was such a slow walker. When we arrived, I built him a nice little house like a doghouse. It had his name on it, and he could sleep in it or sit there when the sun was very hot.

Toby had not been with us very long when one day my sister came into my room, looking very angry.

"That awful tortoise in the garden — is he yours?" she asked.

"Yes. He's called Toby," I said.

"I don't care what he's called," she said, "but he's got to stop eating my strawberries."

"What happened?" I asked.

"I went into the garden to sunbathe, and I took a bowl of wild strawberries with me. Then along comes this Toby thing, and the moment he sees them he tries to climb right into the dish. I moved them to the other side of me, and this Toby thing climbs over me. Look at these red marks he's made on my suntan! Then he fell off my tummy straight into the dish of strawberries and squashed them all. You've got to control him. He's not only ruined all my strawberries, but with all these stripes he's made me look like a zebra."

So I had a serious talk with Toby, and he promised never to do such a thing again.

On his birthday, Roger woke up very early because he was so
excited about his party and his presents. He got two big boxes of
special cookies, a windup mouse to play with, a new brush and
comb, and a big box of chocolates.

In the afternoon we had the party, and what a great party it
was! All my animal friends came to it — Mr. and Mrs. Owl, Mr.
and Mrs. Toad, Mr. and Mrs. Frog, Mr. and Mrs. Snake, Mr. and
Mrs. Butterfly, and many, many more. We had ice cream and
Jell-O and lots of lemonade to drink and crackers to pull and a
big cake covered with pink and white icing and decorated with
five candles.

Afterward we brought the radio outside and danced to the music. Everyone agreed that they had never been to such a terrific birthday party.

The next day, I went to Toby's house. I found him sitting in the doorway, crying his heart out.

"What in the world is the matter?" I asked. "You seemed so happy yesterday."

"I *was*," sobbed Toby, "until I started to think about it."

"About what?" I asked.

"Well, look who was at the party," said Toby. "Mr. and Mrs. Owl, Mr. and Mrs. Toad, Mr. and Mrs. Frog, and so on. But there was only *one* tortoise at your party, and that was *me*. I had no Mrs. Tortoise."

"I see," I said. "So what you want is a lady tortoise?"

"Yes," said Toby excitedly, "so at the next party we can be Mr. and Mrs. Tortoise."

"Well," I said, "I'll see what I can do."

For the next three days, Toby and I, with the help of Roger, searched for a lady tortoise. It was hot work walking through the olive trees, and although we met plenty of tortoises, not one of them was exactly right. They were either too big or too small or their shells were the wrong color or they had some other fault.

"Boy oh boy!" growled Roger. "You *are* difficult to please, Toby."

"I'm sorry," said Toby, "but if we choose just any old tortoise, I'll be unhappy and so will she."

"You're absolutely right," I said. "Let's keep on looking."

On the fourth day, we found her, a beautiful young lady tortoise sitting under an olive tree eating dandelions.

"That's the one!" said Toby excitedly. "Isn't she beautiful?"

"Hello," I said to the lady tortoise. "What's your name?"

"Matilda," she replied through a mouthful of dandelion flowers.

"Well, I'm Gerry. Would you like to come and live with us and our animal friends? You and Toby here will have a lovely house to live in and lots of delicious food to eat."

"That sounds like fun. Can I come and see if I like it first?" Matilda asked Toby.

"Of course," said Toby, and off we went home.

After she had met Mr. and Mrs. Owl, Mr. and Mrs. Toad, Mr. and Mrs. Frog, and all the others, Matilda decided she would stay with Toby. So they got married, and we had a wonderful party, and everyone gave the tortoises lots of wedding presents.

I built them a new, bigger house with "Toby and Matilda" written over the door. As I watched them settle down happily together, I was prouder than ever that we had rescued Toby from the sea, and I told Roger so.

"It's the best day's work we've ever done."

"You're right, you're right," growled Roger in agreement.

First U.S. Edition

ISBN 1-55970-145-5
Library of Congress Catalog Card Number 91-55147
Library of Congress Cataloging-in-Publication information is available.

Published in the United States by Arcade Publishing, Inc., New York,
a Little, Brown company, by arrangement with
Michael O'Mara Books Ltd.

1 3 5 7 9 10 8 6 4 2
Printed in Belgium